THE UNICORN DRUM

Annabel Farjeon

THE UNICORN DRUM

illustrated by
BABETTE COLE

KAYE & WARD
LONDON

First published by Kaye & Ward Ltd
21 New Street, London EC2M 4NT
1976
Text copyright © 1976 Annabel Farjeon
Illustrations and typography © Kaye & Ward

ISBN 0 7182 1025 5

Photoset in Monophoto Baskerville by
Computer Photoset Ltd, Birmingham
Printed in Great Britain by
A Wheaton and Co., Exeter

Haymo's Room

The night watchman was called Haymo. He wore big blue gym shoes with the laces undone, because if he tied them up he couldn't undo the knots. When Haymo trod on the left lace with his right foot he would trip and, like as not, tread on the other lace with the other foot. After a tug of war, his feet would stumble on. To avoid this bother he walked with his feet wide apart.

As he was a night watchman, Haymo slept all day, getting up at five o'clock in the afternoon. This other way round life suited him, for he was happiest in the dark. Bright light made him blink and feel ashamed of his moony face and big body. Children in the town sometimes called after him, "Hi clown!", which made him laugh and wave back. But his face was smiling as well as sad.

The town in which Haymo lived was called Crouch, and the house at the end of the town in which he slept was called Crouch End. It was kept by a lady who fussed about burglars. Although she trusted Haymo, she would not give him a key, thinking he might leave it in the door by mistake. At tea time she always locked up, so that when Haymo wanted to leave for work he had to climb down the drainpipe into the garden. Then he would walk to the centre of Crouch, which was not far. By the time he came back from work the landlady would be up to open the front door for him. She never asked how he left the house each

night and he never told her. The fact was
he liked sliding down the drainpipe.

It was Haymo's job to see that all was safe at Monty's Music Ltd., which was at the back of a block called Hardstone House. The factory made drums, recorders and tambourines. On the main street, in the front part of Hardstone House, there was the sweet shop at one corner, Woolworth's in the middle and a launderette at the other corner.

On duty Haymo's companion was Mincer, a huge, wolf-like dog with ragged grey fur. Mrs Clapper, who owned the sweet shop, kept him all day until Haymo fetched him in the evening.

One cold winter, just before Christmas, Haymo woke in the afternoon as usual and made his breakfast. He boiled an egg in the kettle on the gas ring and then made tea with the same hot water. This saved work. He sat close to the fire to keep warm and at the end of his meal licked his plate. He grinned to think how his landlady would have thrown up her hands in horror.

"Saves washing up," he said aloud, as though she was in the room. "And tastes lovely!"

Haymo often talked like this when he was alone for he was very friendly with himself.

Next he searched round for his old coat that was the colour of rusty iron. It was not hanging in its usual place: on the hook there was only a hot water bottle that leaked, together with his cap and belt. He strapped the belt low round his fat tummy, as though to hold it up, put on the cap and looked about again. On the back of the chair were two socks, one red and one blue.

"Better take the washing. Washing, washing! Where are you?" he called, as if waiting for it to come out of hiding.

Soon a sack was filled with shirts and socks, towels, trousers and pullovers. The socks had hidden themselves all over the place; in the bed, over the fender, mixed with tools and comics. It took a long time to find the coat, which had hidden itself under the bed.

"There you are!" cried Haymo. "Things don't like being looked for. They come back on their own if you don't bother them. If you do they sometimes go away for good."

He opened the window and dropped the sack onto the flowerbed. Then he clambered onto the sill, shut the window, clasped the drainpipe and slid to the ground.

The air was sharp and the sky stiff, like grey cardboard, as he walked into town.

The Launderette

When Haymo reached Hardstone House, with the sack over his back, yellow light was shining from the sweet shop and the launderette. In between, Woolworth's window glittered with silver tinsel and glass balls. He went into the sweet shop.

"Evening Mrs Clapper."

"Good evening, Mr Haymo. Wash night is it?"

"It struck me the time had come," he replied gravely. He studied the cheap sweets and said, "A pair of liquorice bootlaces and a sherbert fizzer for my elevenses, please."

Haymo had his elevenses at night, not in the morning, because of his day being the wrong way round.

"You should learn to tie bows with these bootlaces," Mrs Clapper said, "then you could keep your shoes in order. Mind out – here comes Mincer!"

Mincer had jumped up in the back room when he heard Haymo's voice. With a leap he was over the counter and,

standing on his hind legs, had put his paws round Haymo's neck.

"Hey – hoy! You'll have me over!" cried Haymo.

They tottered about, hugging each other, Mincer licking the wide cheeks with a long pink tongue.

Next they went shopping in the supermarket and then to the launderette, where Haymo soon set the machine going. They sat back, Haymo on the bench, Mincer underneath, to watch the clothes tumble past the glass porthole, red, brown and blue, with a swish of water, then the froth of soap that turned grey as the grime drained out. The washing machine shook and rumbled.

"You would think it was shivering with cold, not hot," Haymo told Mincer. He broke off a length of bootlace and gave it to the dog.

A boy and a girl with ginger hair and round brown eyes turned to look. The boy was about ten, the girl younger. She had a long fat plait. They watched the dog rub the side of his mouth with a paw as the liquorice stuck between his teeth.

"He's not too keen on that bootlace by the faces he's pulling," Haymo said, offering them a piece which he held out like a dangling black worm.

The little girl, with a scared glance at the dog, nodded and took it. Then they all sat and chewed, the liquorice smell thick in the air. No one else came into the launderette.

Suddenly foam rose from the top of a washing machine. Up and up it frothed, through the top, over the edge and down the side in a slippery stream.

15

"Oh dear!" the girl cried. "I told you Tom – you put too much powder in."

"Don't fuss Rene," Tom said calmly. "It's frothing at the mouth like a dragon."

Haymo smiled. "No harm done."

He took out his red cotton hankerchief with white spots and mopped up. Drips plopped onto his gym shoes.

"You should put your hanky in to wash," Rene advised.

"It could do with a spin," Haymo agreed, and did as he was told.

At once the foam behind his porthole turned pink.

Haymo cried, "Lovely strawberry ice cream! Hey – it's going red."

"Oh dear," said Rene. "All your things will come out pink."

"That will make a nice change," he

replied, and they all laughed.

When everyone had settled again, Mincer poked his head up and sniffed at Rene's foot that dangled in mid air. She gave a squeak, her face stiff with fear, and pulled her legs onto the bench. Haymo patted Mincer, in case he was offended.

Tom asked, "Is he all right? He looks wild."

Haymo chuckled. "He's that soppy he would lick a burglar's boots."

Mincer wagged his tail so that it banged on the floor like a hammer.

When all the washing was clean and dry, the children folded their things and put them in a bag. But Haymo stuffed his pink dyed clothes into the sack anyhow.

"Are you going home now?" Rene asked.

"No, I'm off to work."

"To work!" they exclaimed.

So Haymo told them that his job was to guard Monty's Music factory at night.

"But suppose robbers came, wouldn't you be scared?" Rene asked.

"I expect we'd be scared about equal, but I've got the dog. Hey, Mincer, move off my foot, or we'll be late."

Rene stepped away from the dog, behind her brother, and put the end of her plait in her mouth.

Tom asked, "Can we come with you? You see, Mum has gone to look after a sick friend and she won't be in till seven o'clock. I'd love to see the drums. I play the drum at school."

"He really is good," his sister said.

Haymo looked glum. "It's not really allowed."

"I don't want to go with that dog," Rene said.

"You see, Rene's scared of dogs," Tom explained. "They make her go all funny. Couldn't you just take me to see the big drum?"

Haymo smiled his moony smile and swung his sack over his back.

"Right then. Hurry along and I'll ask Mr Monty. Mr Monty's all right if you keep on the right side of him."

Tom swung his bag over his back, too, and grinned.

"Come on, Rene, don't sulk," he said. "The dog won't bite."

"I'm not!" she said sulkily, as they all trooped out of the launderette.

Monty's Music Factory

At the back of Hardstone House there was a courtyard, at the far end of which stood the factory. In one corner an iron staircase led round and round, up to the first floor, and beside it rose a plane tree the branches of which stretched even higher than the factory. In summer the leaves of this tree could be seen from the High Street, waving over the roof like little green flags.

Haymo led the children to the iron stairs.

"We go up the fire escape," he said. "The big doors are locked at night."

"You could climb into that tree from the stairs," Tom said.

"That is just what a burglar did before I came. Hid in the branches and then nipped up the fire escape. Mr Monty wanted to chop it down after that, but he was stopped."

"How?" Tom asked.

"Can't say – I only know we are not allowed to chop it down."

"Did the burglar take anything."

"I should say he did! He opened up the doors, his friend backed up a lorry, and they filled it with drums. You see, the old fellow who had my job would go to the pub of an evening, and these blokes knew. Of course, Mr Monty gave him the sack and that's when I took over."

As they climbed the stairs their shoes rang on the metal treads and echoed back from the brick wall: clang-ang, clang-ang, clang-ang. At the top Haymo banged on the door.

"Where's Mincer?" Tom asked.

"Hey – hoy! Mincer!" Haymo roared.

There was a yelp below and then the scratch of claws pounding up the stairs. Rene pressed herself against the rail as the dog's thick coat brushed her leg. She looked over at the drop to the yard. The tree branches were black as they twisted about, down, down into darkness. She felt dizzy and took hold of Haymo's coat.

"Mincer hates coming up these open stairs," Haymo said. "It makes him tremble to see through, so he takes it at a run."

He banged the door again and with a squeak and a jolt it opened. A young man let them in.

"Hi Haymo!" he said, jigging from

one foot to the other.

"Why, it's Mr Gordon! How did you come to be here?"

"I told Uncle Monty I'd let you in so he could do some Christmas shopping. My group is doing a show in town tonight. Have you seen the posters? The Smilers are Here! We're playing at the Bingo Hall. Who are your friends?"

Tom had pushed by and was gazing up in awe. "Are you Gordon of The Smilers?"

"That's me. Coming to see us? We're only in Crouch one night."

As Tom still gaped, Rene explained, "Mum wouldn't let him go. She said it went on too late."

"Rotten shame!" Gordon said.

Haymo took Rene's hand. "You leave the washing here and I'll show you

24

round. This floor is just a store for wood and stuff."

He led the way down some stairs to a great room where long metal tubes twisted about the ceiling: they looked like giant snakes in the one dim light that was left on at night.

Gordon Smiler took over. "See – this is where they bend the hoops that fit over the drum heads: big ones for bass drums, little ones for side drums." He pointed to piles of wooden rings. "I used to work here, so I know all about it."

"What's that pretty stuff?" Rene asked, pulling Haymo.

"Those are sheets of plastic. They fit round the outside of drums to make them look smart. Those are piles of finished basses." He pointed to a high pyramid. "I always think they look like tins in a supermarket for giants. But stocks are low now, being Christmas. There's just this special order complete: the only set in the whole world."

They stood before a drum set in which each drum was painted with a beautiful

unicorn standing on his hind legs under a tree dotted with oranges. The unicorn had a beard and a twisted horn.

"Oh it's lovely!" Rene cried. "Tom would like that for Christmas."

"That would cost your Mum a packet," Haymo laughed. "Come and see my den."

Gordon was showing Tom how a drum-pedal worked, but when he saw Haymo go into the den he said, "Well, I must be off. Mustn't be late. You tell Haymo I let myself out."

He fingered the tenor drum of the Unicorn set. Tom still could not take his eyes from the young man. What luck. He'd be able to tell his friends at school that he actually knew Gordon of The Smilers.

"Run along!" Gordon said sharply.

Tom walked towards the den, then stopped to look back once more. To his surprise he saw Gordon had moved the big bass drum and was lifting the tenor drum from its stand.

Gordon tucked the drum under his arm, glanced up and saw the boy with his mouth open. For a moment he also stood still, then he called Tom back in a whisper.

"Here – come here! I'll let you into a secret. But don't you say a word to anyone. I am just borrowing this drum for tonight. Mine got broken coming here in the van. Now don't you split on me, will you?"

Tom asked in wonder, "But why don't you just ask your uncle if you can take it?"

Gordon gave a soft laugh. "Ask Uncle

Monty! Don't be funny! He wouldn't lift a finger if all my drums rolled over a cliff. You keep mum and I'll give you a free ticket next time we're in Crouch. Sssh! Keep that dog under control. Don't

worry, I'll bring it back after the show. Bye!" He waved and hurried off.

Tom stood there till he heard the door to the fire escape grate and then quick steps running down the stairs.

Mincer's Tail

"Look at this neat little cooker!" Haymo was saying. "I can fry up me midnight dinner a treat. No one to moan about smelling the place out with chips and sausages. Chair's comfy too. Electric clock to tell me the time and a rug for Mincer. Some firms give you the telly, but myself I prefer to think."

Rene asked, "Don't you get frightened all alone?"

"Why should I? Mincer keeps me company. We play hide and seek when everyone else is in bed. He loves that – goes beserk."

"It's so dark and spooky," Rene said.

Haymo spoke in his slow gentle voice. "I'm very fond of the dark: it's cosy. You see, I'm a man who likes his own company. I expect you prefer lots of noisy friends?"

Rene laughed and touched his hand.

"Where's that brother of yours? Your Mum will be wondering where you two have got to."

At this moment Tom pushed the door open. Rene at once saw an odd look on his face.

He spoke crossly. "Come on, we'd better go. And – and Gordon said to tell you he was late for the gig, so he went."

Mincer stalked up to Tom, sniffed his hand and then wandered out into the factory.

Rene gazed at Haymo's kindly face. "I'm going to bring you a present tomorrow," she said.

"A present! That's very kind, but it isn't my birthday you know,"

"But it is Christmas."

"Oh – ah – yes, I'd forgotten. It's so long since – " he stopped short as a drum beat sounded. Boom! Then again: boom! boom! boom! The children turned pale.

"Who's banging that bass?" Haymo shouted, as he strode out into the dim workshop.

Rene clutched her brother's arm and whispered, "Do you think it's a ghost?" Tom did not reply. He wondered if Gordon Smiler had thought better of taking the drum and brought it back.

Boom! boom! boom! went the drum again, sounding through the silence.

Then they heard Haymo call, "Just

come and look at this!"

They ran out to see Mincer standing by the big drum Gordon had moved. He wagged his tail and with every swish it banged the drum head: boom! boom! boom! He gazed at Haymo. All at once the night watchman turned and looked about, as though seeking something. His face was puzzled.

"It's gone," he said. "That's what Mincer was telling me – it's gone."

"What's gone?" Rene asked.

But Tom knew. His face turned red with shame and he wished he was miles away from Monty's Music factory.

Haymo shook his head back and forth, back and forth. "That's bad – very bad," he said. You two had better be off. I may have to call in Mr Monty. Gordon must have nicked that tenor drum."

Slowly he led the way up to the store room to show the children out.

Though he longed to, Tom did not dare to speak. At the last moment, when the door was open, he said, "It wasn't your fault, anyway."

"That drum set is the only one of its kind in the whole world. And it was all ready to be sent off. Mr Monty will be hopping mad. Gordon always was a one for tricks. Once he tied all my shoe laces together when I wasn't looking and I took a header when I tried to walk. Got two black eyes that time. Gordon always liked his joke. He'll get me the sack I shouldn't wonder."

They stood on the fire escape.

"It wasn't a joke," Tom said grimly, as he dragged the washing bag. "I saw him take it. It was because his tenor drum got broken. He told me he needed it just for tonight."

There was silence as Haymo took this in.

"So that's it," he said at last. "I shouldn't have left him alone – not for one minute."

"He said he'd bring it back after the show."

"Let's hope he does. You buzz off. I must sort this out."

The worried look did not leave Haymo's face as he returned to his den. He rubbed his hair into a tangle, then took from his carrier bag milk, sausages, bread and his knitting, which he had brought along with the washing, but had not washed. It was a long, wobbly, orange scarf. But he was too bothered to knit, so he just sat.

After an hour Haymo went and stood at the top of the iron stairs in the cold night. From the Bingo Hall he could hear the blare of a trumpet, the clang of an electric guitar and the beat of drums. He liked the sound and would have stayed longer had he not felt so worried about the unicorn drum. Then, with Mincer at his heels, he did a round of the factory, shining a torch on locks and bolts to make sure they were fast. He also made sure Gordon had not taken anything else. When he listened for The Smilers again there was the sound of cheers and the music went on.

Back in his den Haymo knitted three rows of the scarf, but found a stitch had dropped. He was afraid to pick it up, lest it ran right down to the bottom. He would have to ask Mrs Clapper for help tomorrow: she always helped with his knitting. It was only thinking of the red-headed children that cheered him.

"We must stop Rene being scared of you," he told Mincer. "Let's make dinner."

They shared fried sausages, fried bread and sweet tea.

The hands of the clock were on midnight when Haymo went up to the fire escape again. The town was quiet. A few flakes of snow fell. He heard steps in the street below. Nearer and nearer they came, till it seemed they must be in the courtyard. Must be Gordon, he thought, but he could see nothing in the dark. The steps began to fade away and Haymo went back to his den and sat hunched over the electric fire, hoping that Gordon would turn up with the unicorn drum, but no one came.

Mr Monty Gets Cross

At eight o'clock the next day Haymo let in his boss. Mr Monty was a little old man, with a face like a sheep wearing glasses. He stamped snow off his boots and wagged a finger.

"You're looking very grave Haymo," he said. "Cheer up: Christmas tomorrow, and I'll be bringing in your hamper tonight."

Haymo was to guard the factory over Christmas, just as he did at weekends. He did not mind this, for he had no family to visit and was happy to stay there with Mincer.

But now he shook his head. "An awkward thing happened after you left last night." Then he told how Tom had seen Gordon take the unicorn drum.

Mr Monty frowned, pinched his chin and grunted.

"You should never have let those kids in, it's against the rules," he said. "May be they took the drum – hid it in their wash bag. You've been a fool, and I can't afford to have fools here. How can I get another drum in time? If it wasn't that set, it wouldn't matter." He smacked his fist into his hand. "How am I to get it back in time? It was being flown off in three days. A nice mess you've made, letting those kids in!"

"Those kids didn't take it," Haymo said.

"Have you got X-ray eyes? How do you know the boy wasn't telling a lie about Gordon? The Smilers left town

last night. You're no good as a watchman—you're fired! You can have a weeks wages and out!"

Sadly Haymo left the factory. Mincer walked behind quietly when he saw his master's face.

"I'm in the soup," Haymo told Mrs Clapper.

"You poor thing!" she cried, when she had heard all. "Still, it was a bit of luck having that boy, for now you know who took the drum."

"I don't think Mr Monty liked to own up to his own nephew playing that trick. If I knew where Gordon was I could fetch it back."

"It wasn't fair, giving you the sack. Mr Monty should have known better than to leave Gordon in the place. He stopped working there long ago because of some prank he played." Mrs Clapper tossed her head and the frills on her blouse shook too.

42

"You see, Gordon needed that tenor drum for his concert," Haymo said, by way of excuse for the young man.

"He should have gone without!" Mrs Clapper cried. "And now what do we do about Mincer? He'll be broken hearted."

"I'll come back this evening and we will fix something," Haymo said, though he had no idea what. "By-the-bye, I dropped a stitch in my knitting and hadn't the heart to pick it up. Would you do me the favour of catching it again?"

Mrs Clapper smiled. "Of course, Mr Haymo! Just you leave it with me."

It happened that while Haymo was asleep at Couch End that morning, Tom and Rene paid a visit to the sweet shop.

"Can we have some bootlaces please," Rene said.

Mrs Clapper stared hard. "Are you the two children who were with Mr Haymo yesterday?" she asked.

"Yes. Do you know him?" Rene replied.

"Did you take that drum from the factory?"

Tom glared. "Of course not! It was Gordon Smiler. Didn't he bring it back?"

Then Mrs Clapper told them that Gordon had gone away with the drum and Mr Monty had given Haymo the sack.

"But they haven't gone!" Rene cried. "We saw the Smilers just now. Their van is parked outside the Bingo Hall being loaded."

"Yes, they were packing their kit in." Tom's face turned pink as an idea came.

"Come on Rene, let's see if we can catch them? Quick!"

And the two children raced out of the shop.

Tom Gone

Gordon Smiler did not mean to steal the drum from his uncle, he only meant to keep it till New Years' day, when his own drum would be mended. His van was parked by the back entrance to the Bingo Hall. It was painted with purple and green blobs, on which THE SMILERS was written many times. When Tom and Rene ran round the corner they saw a young man was helping Gordon to pack. They stopped short to watch, then slowly walked on. When they came level with the van the two young men had gone inside the hall again. There was no one about.

Tom peered in at the loud speakers and stood on tiptoe to see over the bass drum.

"Can you see it?" Rene asked.

"No, I can't. Ooh yes, there's the unicorn, up at the front. I'll have to climb over everything."

"What if somebody comes?"

"Just sing if they do," Tom replied. "You ought to whistle, but we all know you can't."

He was up in the van before Rene could answer. She stood trembling with fright, but no one came. She could see Tom on all fours near the unicorn drum.

Suddenly the two men ran out of the hall. Gordon slammed the back of the van shut, locked the doors, leapt into the front of the van and drove off with his friend.

47

OGDENS PIES
ARE THE BEST
GORDON AND THE SMILERS
TONITE
HALL
CROUCH
F.C.
RULE O.K.
AND THE
SMILERS

Rene had no time to do more than gasp. But as the van moved she dashed forward and was in time to see it swing into the main street and away. She stood at the corner not knowing what to do. Mum was at work and Tom had been carried off. She rushed along the High Street in a panic, bumping into people, pushing, shoving, past the launderette, past Woolworths and into Mrs Clapper's shop. There she stopped, tried to speak, but her words were drowned in a flood of tears.

Mrs Clapper took Rene behind the counter and into her back room, which was piled high with boxes of cigarettes and sweets. There, between sobs, the story was told. When Rene came to the end, the shop bell clanged.

Mrs Clapper gave Rene a pat. "Now

don't you fret. I'll think up something while I serve my customer. You wait here like a good girl and I'll be back in a jiffy."

Rene sank to the floor and tears ran down her cheeks, as she wondered if she would ever see her brother again. She felt something wet on her hand and looking up, saw it was Mincer licking her fingers. He seemed so sorry and so kind that Rene touched his ear. He came closer. Then she put her arms round his neck and hugged his head. His furry coat tickled her nose, and as he nuzzled her a lovely doggy smell spread.

"Oh Mincer!" cried Rene, feeling much better.

Mincer licked her face and sat down. His tail thumped the floor and he put a paw in her lap. They sat like this till Mrs

Clapper came back.

"I've thought," she said, slowly lowering herself into her armchair with a shake, as a bird settles on its nest. "You ask Haymo: he will know where to find Gordon Smiler. You take Mincer, he knows the way. The house is at the end of Lumber Lane it's called Crouch End. And cross the road with other people – not by yourself. Of course, Haymo may be asleep, but never mind, just wake him up."

Rene put her hand on the dog's neck. "Will Mincer come with me?"

"I dare say, if you ask him nicely."

So she bent over and whispered, "Will you come to find Haymo please?"

The dog wagged his tail and they went out into the snowy street.

On reaching the last house in Lumber

Lane, Mincer dashed in at the gate and barked. Rene hung back, afraid to knock on the door. When she raised her arm it would not reach the knocker and there was no bell. But Mincer barked again at which a window above them was pushed open and Haymo's head poked out.

"I knew it was you the first time," Haymo said to the dog. "Hold on and I'll be down."

When he opened the front door he whispered, "Lucky he barked. She would never have opened up if you'd knocked: she's scared of burglars."

They crept up the stairs to Haymo's room. He had been polishing his brass candlestick and his copper kettle, till they shone like gold in the dingy room. A pile of pink tinted washing lay in the corner.

"Mrs Clapper said you might be asleep," Rene said.

"I didn't feel much like sleep after I got the sack. So I said to myself, you polish the brass and make things cheerful for Christmas."

Rene thought of Christmas without her brother: tears ran down her cheeks.

"Hey – hoy! What's up?" Haymo cried. "You mustn't do that. You tell me."

So once again Rene told the story. Haymo's wide, pale face looked grave, but at the end a slow grin spread across his cheeks. At once Rene felt better.

"You and me and Mincer will see what can be done. We must find Gordon. He's not a bad lad, only thoughtless." Haymo lifted the kettle and rubbed it with his sleeve. "Now that's what I call a lovely shine." He held it near her face. "Can you see your nose in my kettle? The dents make it look all funny."

Rene laughed when she saw her wobbly face in the copper mirror.

Haymo went on, "Now creep down stairs very soft. We can't go the other way because I think Mincer would find sliding down the drainpipe tricky."

On the Move

Tom hid behind the bass drum as the van rattled up the High Street. A music stand clinked, the engine raced, and the boys sang The Smilers' theme song.

Gordon tooted his horn and shouted, "We'll pack properly at the other end."

Their journey was not long: they stopped in Lumber Lane and the young men jumped out of the van, slamming the doors behind them, and ran into a house.

Tom at once took up the unicorn drum and scrambled out. He just had time to rush into the garden of the house next door when the two Smilers came

back with their suit cases and began to re-pack the kit. Tom crept behind a bush and watched.

"Where's that tenor drum, Gordon?" one shouted.

"Up front," Gordon yelled back.

"It isn't you know."

"It is you know. Take another look, Roger."

Then there was a lot of talk. Roger said the drum must have been left in the Bingo Hall.

"Could anyone have nicked it?" someone asked.

Tom shivered with fright. A blob of snow fell down the back of his neck. He shivered with cold and moved the drum so that the glint of its metal would not catch the light. At last the Smilers all got in the van and drove off.

Had he known it, Tom was just a few yards from Crouch End and could have given the drum to Haymo there and then, but now his aim was to take it back to the factory. He took off his jacket and put it round the drum to try and hide it. He wondered where Rene was and thought she must have gone home: the key was under the stone by the back door. He thought he would go home first and so turned down a side street. This was why he did not meet his sister and Mincer, who were just going to see Haymo.

When Tom found that Rene was not at home he grew worried. He put the drum in a big bag, glad to have his coat on again, and ran out, slamming the back door behind him. Then he stood still, remembering. He had left the key inside. This meant they could not go home till Mum got back at six. Where would they go all day? Anyway, he must find his sister first, for she was only just eight and he had to look after her.

Tom set off for the Bingo Hall, where he had left Rene but, on rounding the corner, he saw The Smilers' purple and green van parked at the back door. There was no sign of Rene. He turned and made for the sweet shop, dashing in so that his bag knocked against the wall. The drum let out a hollow boom, as Tom found himself standing between two young men: Roger and Gordon.

At that moment Mrs Clapper was saying, "I'll just fetch them for you." She went into the back room.

The boom of the drum made Gordon turn. He stared.

"Aren't you the one – yes – and I do

believe it was you – yes –!"

Tom turned white: he could not speak. The drummer in his black jacket and blue boots with stars on them, looked huge.

"What have you got in there?" Gordon asked.

As the boy made no reply, he took the bag and looked in, then whistled. "You little thief! The minute I heard that drum I guessed. You thief!"

"I'm not!" Tom cried, hoping Mrs Clapper would come back.

The young men stood close each side of him.

"You cheeky brat!" Roger said angrily. He pushed Tom towards the door. "You come with me!"

"I didn't steal it! It was Gordon – he did!"

But The Smilers had the drum once more and there was nothing Tom could do.

Gordon spoke to his friend. "You stay and get the fags, Roger, while I deal with this problem."

He shoved Tom forward, for he wanted the boy out of the shop before Mrs Clapper saw them.

Tom wriggled and squeaked, "Don't! Stop it! I didn't!"

But as Gordon pushed, the door opened and Haymo's big body blocked the way.

The Nifty Kid

Haymo stood in the doorway and stared.

Tom cried quickly, "I got it, but he's taken it back."

"You let go of that kid," Haymo said quietly to Gordon.

But Gordon clung on to Tom's arm. Haymo looked bothered.

"Why didn't you tell me you wanted the drum Gordon?" he asked. "Mr Monty's going beserk. Why didn't you bring it back last night?"

"I needed it for a couple more gigs – then I was going to bring it back," Gordon replied sulkily. "Honest, Haymo, I need it tonight."

"But Mr Monty needs that drum now. He has to send that set off by plane. It's a special order. You should have told me. We might have mended your drum by now."

Then Mrs Clapper's voice came high and sharp. "You got Mr Haymo the sack. Did you know that? It's a crying shame."

Tom felt Gordon let go of his arm and

at once he dived between Haymo's legs and was out of the door, past Rene and Mincer, and down the street.

Haymo said, "You see, I have to take that drum back."

"You must be joking," Roger mocked.

"It's not yours," Haymo went on.

"Come and get it then!" Gordon laughed, waving the bag.

For a moment the night watchman was puzzled, but when he stepped forward, Gordon threw the bag over his head to Roger, who caught it neatly and rushed out of the door.

Haymo grasped Gordon and together they bumped a shelf of sweets, causing two jars to fall and break with a clatter. Bull's eyes and pear drops skidded across the floor. Mrs Clapper cried out. Now the door swung open and Mincer bounded in, with Rene behind. The minute the dog saw Gordon attacking Haymo he gave a growl and sank his teeth into Gordon's boot.

"Stop!" shouted the drummer. "Take that dog off!"

Haymo let go of his arm and called Mincer off.

"You fetch that drum back," Haymo said.

"I'll call the police if you don't," Mrs Clapper added.

"Look what that dog has done to my best boot!" Gordon moaned. "How about if I bring the drum back after the show tomorrow?"

Mrs Clapper saw her friend waver. She said, "No, make him bring it back right now. Don't be a softy Mr Haymo."

Gordon watched Mincer lick up a pear drop. His way to the door was clear.

"Right you are! See you soon!" he called cheekily.

Haymo stepped forward, but his left

shoe lace caught under his right foot. He slipped on a bull's eye and fell.

Gordon stopped in the doorway. "Give my love to Uncle Monty," he sang out and raced off to the van, where he knew Roger would be waiting.

Indeed, there sat Roger, ready to be driven off, with the drum in its bag safe on his lap. Gordon leapt in, laughing, and started the engine.

"I left poor old Haymo floored," he said.

"Hurry up or they'll be after us."

The van moved with a jolt. Gordon groaned and pulled up. "It's a flat tyre! Of all the bad luck! Come on, we'll have to change the wheel in record time."

They ran to the back and saw the tyre squashed flat on the road.

"Funny thing," said Gordon, "It must

be a nail – or – or – maybe that kid let the air out."

They had the nuts undone, the jack lifted the axle high, tipping the van. The wheel was rolled away and Roger had the spare ready. Then down came the van. Gordon gave the nuts a final turn and the tools were collected.

Roger was pleased. "I would say we did that in three minutes flat. Nearly as good as a racing team."

They ran to the front and jumped in.

"Oh my giddy aunt!" was the next cry. "It's gone again!"

They stared at the seat where Roger had left the bag. Then Gordon grinned.

"The joke is on us. It seems I wasn't meant to have that unicorn drum."

Roger added, "It must have been that nifty little kid. He let down the tyre and

then nabbed the drum while we were at the back. He did a neat job. I wouldn't mind having him on my side. Come on, we're late. You'll have to do without."

Gordon nodded as he moved the gear lever. He felt a good deal of relief, for the thought that Haymo had lost his job because of him had not been a happy one.

Homeless

When Tom raced back into the sweet shop his cheeks were burning.

Rene held a red pear drop to the light and said, "Look, that's Tom's face," and popped it into her mouth.

They had been picking up the sweets, while Mrs Clapper stood, dust pan in hand, ready to sweep up the broken glass. There was a strong smell of pear drops in the shop.

"I've got it, I've got it!" cried Tom. "Look!" He lifted the unicorn drum out of the bag and held it up.

"Isn't that pretty," said Mrs Clapper. Then she added firmly, "Now, Mr

Haymo, you and Mincer take that drum round to Mr Monty at once. Quick sharp! Those boys may be back any time and I don't want more fights."

"Hey – hoy! Mincer!" Haymo called.

"And drop that bull's eye you bad dog or you'll be sick," Mrs Clapper added.

Rene gazed up at the night watchman. "Mr Haymo, would you mind if I did your laces for you?"

They all laughed as Haymo stood with his feet well apart while she tied his laces.

As soon as he was gone, Mrs Clapper told the children to wait in her back room, for she did not want Tom to meet The Smilers just now. She was kept busy selling boxes of chocolates with satin bows, jelly babies, toffees and fizzers, in fact everything for Christmas. For a long time Tom and Rene sat listening to the ring of the till.

"We must give him a Christmas present," Rene said at last. "I don't suppose he gets many."

"What about money?" Tom said.

"If we had colours and paper I could do a lovely picture."

"But we haven't got any money."

"We've got the dinner money."

Tom was doubtful. He had money for fish and chips and his mother trusted him. But they had both eaten so many pear drops that neither felt very hungry.

"Tell you what, we'll buy one lot of fish and chips."

As The Smilers had not come back, Mrs Clapper let the children go to Woolworths next door. Here they found felt pens and a big scrap book, which used up half the money. There was not much left in the shop, cardboard boxes were piled about and paper rustled over the floor. Everything looked dusty and muddled.

On an almost empty counter Rene saw a glass ball: it was blue and shiny, like a peacock's tail, and as large as a man's fist.

"Ooh!" Rene cried. "Let's buy him that."

She pulled at Tom's sleeve, for he was busy tilting a switch-back railway, whose rails were bent so that the train fell off when it came down the hill. Tom turned his head slowly, but when he saw the blue glass ball, he understood.

"How much – how much is it?" Rene asked.

There were two tickets in the tray: one

for 10p, the other for 20p.

A girl spoke sharply, "Don't touch, they're easily broken."

Tom took all the money from his pocket and counted. There was only 15p left.

"If it's 10p we could have chips for dinner," he said.

"It doesn't matter about dinner," Rene said in a grand voice.

But Tom knew she would be hungry later. "If you promise not to be cross because of no dinner we might buy it."

"Of course I won't," Rene said angrily.

"Promise?"

Rene stamped her foot. "Of course I promise!"

The girl behind the counter smiled. "Well, perhaps it is 10p." She wrapped the ball in tissue paper.

"Would you pack it in a box, please. It is a special present," Rene said.

When the children came back to the sweet shop, which was still full of people, Mrs Clapper spoke sharply.

"Run along home or you'll catch your death of cold. And see your sister eats a good dinner, Tom."

It was plain they were not wanted, so they went out and stood in the cold street, where the snow was melting to slush.

Tom owned up. "I've done an awful thing, I shut the back door and the key got left inside by mistake. So we can't go home till Mum gets back."

Rene's face turned glum. "You are silly. I want to draw a picture for Haymo. You are a silly little boy." She tossed her head in scorn.

"Shut up! You do silly things too," Tom snapped back. "Anyway we can sit in the launderette and pretend we're washing."

'Silly little boy," Rene said again.

"I'm not!"

"You are!"

"You said you wouldn't be cross, so there!"

"I'm not!"

"Who's making a sulky face? Anyway, I'm going to buy some chips."

They shared a bag of chips, quarrelled again about who had taken most, and so went to spend the afternoon with the washing machines very displeased with each other.

Mr Monty's Hamper

It was lucky that Haymo saw his friends in the launderette a little later. Rene sat astride the bench, colouring a picture and chewing the end of her plait, so that it looked as if she had a ginger moustache. Tom sat and kicked at the wall with the toe of his damp shoe. His picture had gone wrong, so he just gaped at other peoples' washing, nodded his head and kicked the wall.

Rene said, "Stop joggling." The plait fell from her mouth as she spoke. She put it back and took a purple pen.

Tom said, "Shan't!"

U.D.—F

Then they heard Haymo's kindly voice. "Yours must be a very clean family."

"It isn't," Tom replied. "We can't go home. The back door key got left inside by mistake."

Rene shut her scrap book quickly, so Haymo should not see.

"What time does your Mum get home?"

"Six o'clock. She might be late because of Christmas Eve."

"Then you had best come along with me. Mr Monty wants to meet you two."

All the workers at the music factory had gone home at noon, so that the place was empty once more. Up the iron stairs they climbed beside the plane tree, whose bark shimmered with the wet, melted snow. Black spikey balls dangled from the branches, and Rene lent over the rail to pick one.

"Rolled up hedgehogs, I call them," Haymo said.

The door was opened by Mr Monty, with Mincer panting behind his legs, for he had not liked being left. The dog put his front paws round Haymo's neck and they staggered about for a bit.

Mr Monty grinned his sheepish grin and said to Tom, "I want to hear all about it. Was it you fetched back the unicorn drum?"

Rene glanced at her brother and said, "Sometimes he is quite clever, like about letting air out of tyres. Only he is not much good at painting pictures. When I grow up I'm going to paint like that unicorn on the drum."

"I might even give you a job here,"

Mr Monty said.

Rene was so pleased at this idea that she turned pink and grinned wide.

Mr Monty locked his fingers and then stretched them up to make a row of Xs. He ducked his head and stared at the floor as he spoke. "I wanted to say thanks to you kids. And Haymo has his job back and is willing to see us safe over Christmas. So that's all right. The hamper is in the den, and something for that fool of a dog. But don't you let Gordon in if he calls."

Haymo gazed at his boss with his head on one side. "These kids are locked out, Mr Monty. Can they stay here till six?"

"You know the rule—no strangers. But I think we may say they're not strangers any more."

As soon as Mr Monty had left, they

went to the den and opened the hamper. It was, in fact, a big cardboard box filled with a Christmas dinner that would last Haymo for a week. A brown turkey, cooked by Mrs Monty, with two sorts of stuffing, was tucked up in silver paper. There were tins of baked beans, carrots, potatoes and fruit salad.

"Not rotten small tins like we have," Tom said.

Also there were tins of dog food, a big bone and a box of dates.

Haymo laughed happily. "It strikes me you had better help me out with this lot. Mustn't let it go bad. How about a game of hide and seek first, to get us hungry, and then dinner?"

This seemed a good idea, so Haymo went to hide, while Mincer and the children counted up to a hundred.

"Coming – we're coming!" they called as they ran about the factory, now dim in the fading light. It was Mincer who caught Haymo creeping along the wall behind the pyramid of bass drums.

When Haymo said it was Mincer's turn, Rene asked if she could hide with him, as she did not like to be in the dark by herself. So they went and crouched beside the unicorn drum set.

Tom began to count as fast as he could, but at thirty-two Haymo said, "Mincer and me don't bother to count. We are not much good at sums." So he cried, "Coming!" very loud, and the word echoed.

Mincer and Rene crouched so low they were not seen. Haymo went to the upper floor, while Tom walked between the metal lathes turning knobs.

Rene hugged the dog's neck and kissed his whiskery cheek. "They can't find us," she whispered.

Mincer wagged his tail. Boom! boom! boom! went the bass drum.

At once there were shouts and quick steps and Tom was only just able to touch his sister before she got home.

When it was dinner time Rene thought of the presents. Tom gave the glass ball and Rene gave her picture, which showed a green tree with a purple squiggle for the stairs and a man and a dog at the top. It read: To dere Haymo and Minser a hapy Xmas from Rene.

"She's not much good at spelling," Tom said.

"Better than Mincer or me," Haymo replied. "See him wagging his tail there. I shall pin this over my bed in Lumber

Lane and put this ball on the mantle shelf."

Next they opened the tins and cut the turkey. Sheets of coloured plastic made plates. Rene chose silver, Tom red, while Haymo and Mincer had blue.

"Square plates make a nice change," Haymo said, sharing out the turkey. "Now dive into that tin with a teaspoon. Baked beans are very good cold." He bit at his turkey leg for a time and then asked, "By-the-bye Tom, how did you let down Gordon's tyre?"

"What you do is you push a nail into the valve thing and the air comes out – psssh!"

The night watchman nodded and smiled. "I can see you know about cars."

Rene held up a mince pie. "There's just one. I think Mincer should have it."

"Of course, Mincemeat is his proper name," Haymo replied. "Hey–hoy, look at the way he gobbles!"

So it was that when Tom and Rene got back home they needed no supper. But, before they went to bed, both talking at the same time, they told their mother all about the unicorn drum.